Because the beginning shall remind us of the end
And the first Coming of the second Coming.

T. S. Eliot

The Christmas Miracle

by J. Harold Gwynne

An *ideals* Publication

ACKNOWLEDGMENTS

A CHRISTMAS CAROL by G. K. Chesterton. Reprinted from FIFTY CHRISTMAS POEMS FOR CHILDREN by Florence B. Hyett, by permission of D. Appleton-Century Co., N.Y. JOSEPH by Grace Noll Crowell. Used by permission of Reid Crowell. ONLY AN HOUR by Robinson Jeffers. Copyright 1941 by Robinson Jeffers. Reprinted through courtesy of Donnan C. and Garth S. Jeffers. STAR OF THE NATIVITY by Boris Pasternak. From THE POEMS OF DOCTOR ZHIVAGO by Boris Pasternak, translation © 1971 by Eugene M. Kayden. Used through courtesy of the Estate of Eugene M. Kayden. THE MEANING OF CHRISTMAS by Fulton J. Sheen. From the writings of Bishop Fulton J. Sheen. Copyright by Fulton J. Sheen. Used with permission of the author. THE INN THAT MISSED ITS CHANCE by Amos Russel Wells. Reprinted from THE CHRISTIAN ENDEAVOR WORLD and used by permission.

ISBN 0-89542-046-5 395

Copyright © 1978 by Ideals Publishing Corporation
Printed in the United States of America

Published by Ideals Publishing Corporation
11315 Watertown Plank Road
Milwaukee, Wis. 53226

Editorial Director, James Kuse
Managing Editor, Ralph Luedtke
Photographic Editor, Gerald Koser
Production Editor, Stuart Zyduck

Designed by Patricia Pingry
Artwork by Bruce Bond

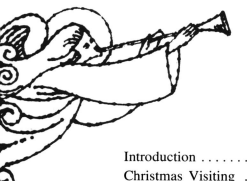

Contents

Introduction

The proper spiritual observance of the Advent and Christmas season is being emphasized more and more by the churches of Christendom. And this is a most timely and encouraging emphasis! For many centuries, the church failed to observe a day of Christmas at all and so neglected to explore and proclaim the rich spiritual truths of the Christmas Gospel to each new generation.

In this eighth decade of our twentieth century, the super emphasis upon the commercial and material side of Christmas is threatening to inundate and obliterate the profound and precious spiritual values of the sacred season. Hence, it is of the utmost importance that we endeavor to recover, appropriate and preserve the invaluable treasures of the Gospel of Christ's Nativity.

The sacred season of Advent and Christmas may well be a season of preparation, expectation and hope centered in the Incarnation of the Son of God. It is our hope that the messages of this volume, if read thoughtfully and devotionally during the days of Advent, will help the reader to come to a deeper understanding of the mystery and meaning of Christmas and to know the certainty of the "good tidings of great joy" of which the herald angel spoke.

J. Harold Gwynne

Painting opposite:
MOTHER AND CHILD
Sandro Botticelli
(Photo, Three Lions, Inc.)

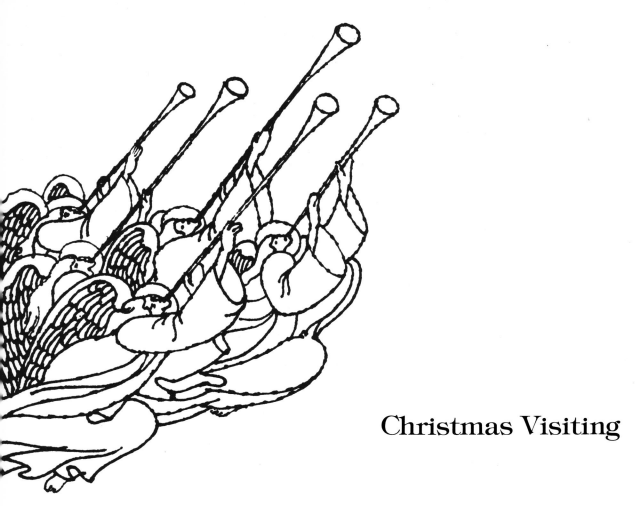

Christmas Visiting

Christmas is essentially a fact of divine visitation. It is the great crisis in history when God comes into human life in the person of his only begotten Son. It celebrates the incarnation of Jesus Christ, the Lord of glory. Christmas is a glorious revelation of the mysteries of the spiritual world; a great demonstration of supernatural signs and wonders. It is the better Jacob's ladder let down from heaven to bring the real presence and blessing of God into human life. We cannot know the meaning of Christmas unless we recognize the reality of these elements from the spiritual world.

What is the nature of these divine visitations of which the Christmas story is so full? The six instances of divine visitation are all visits of angels to men and women: to Zacharias, to Mary and Joseph, to the shepherds. These angels are messengers from God bearing tidings of great importance to God's people. To Zacharias is brought the message concerning the promised birth of John, the forerunner of the Messiah. Mary hears the message concerning the miraculous conception and birth of the Son of the Most High. Joseph receives repeated messages of counsel and guidance for the protection of his sacred charge. The shepherds hear the wonderful message concerning the Savior's birth and the heavenly music of glory and peace.

These angelic visitors come to announce and reveal the plan, purpose and will of God. They come to declare and proclaim what is to come to pass. They brook no argument; they suffer no change of plan; they permit no delay. With sovereign majesty and divine authority, they fulfill their mission as spokesmen of the Most High:

> I am Gabriel, that stand in the presence of God; and am sent to
> speak unto thee, and to show thee these glad tidings . . . The Holy

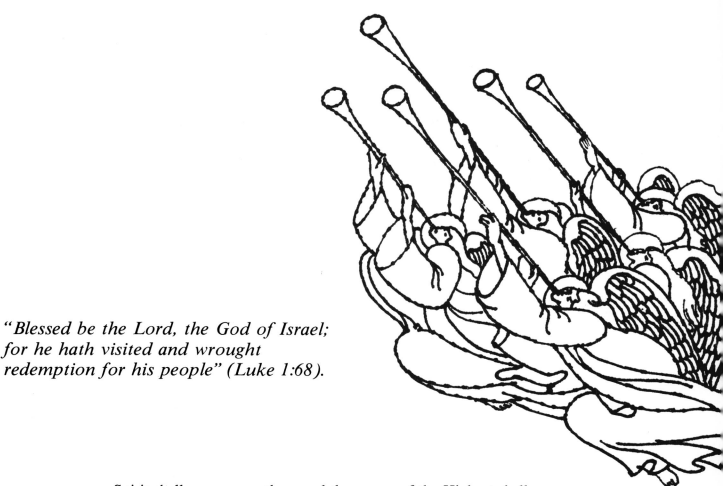

"Blessed be the Lord, the God of Israel; for he hath visited and wrought redemption for his people" (Luke 1:68).

Spirit shall come upon thee, and the power of the Highest shall overshadow thee: therefore also that holy thing which shall be born of thee shall be called the Son of God . . . for with God nothing shall be impossible.

Another form of divine visitation is seen in the supernatural signs. The birth of John to the aged Elisabeth was a supernatural event. The smiting of Zacharias for his unbelief was such a sign. The revelation to Mary of the coming motherhood of Elisabeth was a sign given to strengthen Mary's faith in the promise given. The herald angel gave the shepherds a sign by which they would know the infant Savior: "And this shall be a sign unto you; ye shall find the babe wrapped in swaddling clothes, lying in a manger." To the Wise Men was granted the sign of Jacob's star to start them on their quest, and the guiding light of the star of Bethlehem to bring them to their journey's end. In all these ways, God manifested himself to his people to aid them and guide them in the accomplishment of their mission and the fulfillment of his plans.

But all these things are incidental to the central fact of divine visitation in the birth of Jesus Christ, the Son of God. This is the greatest miracle of all—that the eternal Word of God became flesh and dwelt among us. This is the burden of Zacharias' prophecy and the central fact of his message. He is referring to the birth of Jesus as he says:

Blessed be the Lord, the God of Israel; for he hath visited and redeemed his people, and hath raised up a horn of salvation for us in the house of his servant David . . . whereby the dayspring from on high hath visited to give light to them that sit in darkness and in the shadow of death, to guide our feet into the way of peace.

"I am Gabriel that stand in the presence of God . . ." (Luke 1:19).

What is the supreme purpose in this divine visitation? God's purpose in sending his Son is revealed when the angel said to Mary "He shall be great, and shall be called the Son of the Highest; and the Lord God shall give unto him the throne of his father David: and he shall reign over the house of Jacob for ever; and of his kingdom there shall be no end." To Joseph the angel

THE ANNUNCIATION, Leonardo da Vinci

said, ''Thou shalt call his name Jesus: for he shall save his people from their sins.'' To the shepherds the messenger said, ''Be not afraid; for behold, I bring you good tidings of great joy which shall be to all the people: for there is born to you this day in the city of David a Savior, who is Christ the Lord.''

In short, God visited the world in the incarnation of his Son in order that his fatherhood and saviorhood might be fully revealed. This is the heart of the Gospel. ''For God so loved the world, that he gave his only begotten Son, that whosoever believeth in him should not perish, but have everlasting life . . . And this is life eternal, that they might know thee the only true God, and Jesus Christ, whom thou hast sent.''

9

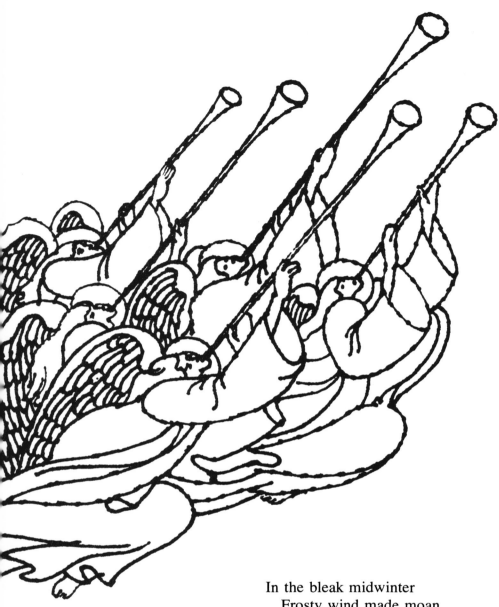

Heaven Cannot Hold Him

In the bleak midwinter
  Frosty wind made moan,
Earth stood hard as iron,
  Water like a stone;
Snow had fallen, snow on snow,
  Snow on snow,
In the bleak midwinter
  Long ago.

Our God, Heaven cannot hold Him
  Nor earth sustain;
Heaven and earth shall flee away
  When He comes to reign:
In the bleak midwinter
  A stable-place sufficed
The Lord God Almighty
  Jesus Christ.

Angels and archangels
    May have gathered there,
Cherubim and seraphim
    Thronged the air;
But only His mother
    In her maiden bliss
Worshiped the Beloved
    With a kiss.

Enough for Him, whom cherubim
    Worship night and day,
A breastful of milk
    And a mangerful of hay;
Enough for Him, whom angels
    Fall down before,
The ox and ass and camel
    Which adore.

What can I give Him,
    Poor as I am?
If I were a shepherd
    I would bring a lamb,
If I were a Wise Man
    I would do my part —
Yet what I can I give Him,
    Give my heart.

Christina Rossetti

" . . . and Jacob begat Joseph the husband of Mary, of whom was born Jesus, who is called Christ" (Matt. 1:16).

Joseph, the Husband of Mary

In many of the great Nativity paintings, Joseph, the husband of Mary appears in the background. He is commonly portrayed as leaning on his staff and gazing with fond affection and tender solicitude upon the virgin and child, the central focus of these paintings. This is as it should be. The angels, the shepherds, the saints, the Wise Men, faithful Joseph and Mary herself are all represented as rendering homage and adoration to the infant Savior.

Joseph is quite commonly regarded as one of the incidental characters of the Gospels. The role he plays in the drama is regarded as a secondary one. He appears in only two of the three scenes that give us glimpses of the Christ Child: at the manger when the shepherds come to worship and in the temple when Simeon and Anna receive the child as Messiah. But Joseph is entirely out of the picture when the Wise Men come to Bethlehem and find Mary and the young child in the house. However, it is far from the truth to say that Joseph is an incidental character and that his part is a minor one.

When God gives a man a definite work to do there can be nothing minor or incidental about it; and the part Joseph plays in the Nativity drama is of the utmost importance. As to his character, Joseph ranks as one of the finest and most noble men of the Bible and deserves to be much better known than he is.

Joseph was spoken of by Matthew as "a righteous man." Although he belonged to the working class, he was of notable ancestry. He was of the house and lineage of David and had the blood of nobility and royalty in his veins. Joseph, however, did not need to depend upon his ancestors for his reputation, for he was a man of eminent character and substantial worth in his own right. The family tree had not yet fallen into decay when Joseph appeared, but rather it yielded some of its finest fruit.

Joseph's secret was his devout faith in God; he faithfully worshiped and served the God of Israel all his life. He had been reared in a godly home, brought up in the faith of his fathers, nurtured in the Scriptures and in the worship of the synagogue. He was one of that peerless company of devout Israelites that have been called "the quiet in the land." In these quiet souls was the real heart of Israel. They did not have a prominent part in the life of the nation as did the scribes, pharisees and Sadducees; but they belonged to that godly remnant that constituted the real hope of the nation.

The purity and strength of Joseph's character was evident when he rendered implicit obedience to the Divine will. God revealed his plans and purposes to Joseph from time to time through his angel who appeared to Joseph in dreams. At each separate appearance, the angel gave Joseph clear and definite instructions as to what he should do. And in each case, Joseph did exactly as the angel of the Lord commanded him. Consequently, God's overruling plan and purpose for the salvation of mankind through the gift of his Son was carried out. The highest privilege and honor that can come to any man came to Joseph: that of being the willing and obedient servant of the Most High.

In Joseph's character we also find expressed the highest type of fatherly love. With beautiful devotion and self-sacrifice, Joseph bestowed the most tender of love upon his young wife and her firstborn son. His chief concern at all times was for their safety and welfare. The holy family—Joseph, Mary and the child Jesus—form a trinity of love: father love, mother love, filial love. Joseph was a good father: kind, loving, generous. As Jesus grew to boyhood and young manhood, he must have found in Joseph his best companion and friend. We know that Jesus was the first to teach that God is our heavenly Father and that God is love. We have every right to think that Jesus found in Joseph an example of the love of God for his children.

The record is silent as to the last days of Joseph. Some think that he may have died before Jesus entered his public ministry. There are only a few indirect references to Joseph in the Gospels, such as the attempts of the unbelieving Jews to identify Jesus as "the carpenter's son." In all probability Joseph died before the crucifixion of Jesus; for at that time, Jesus committed His mother to the care of his apostle John, an act which would not have been necessary had Joseph been alive.

Joseph's highest mission was that of complete devotion to the interests of Christ. Humanly speaking, we could not have the Christmas gospel of the Babe of Bethlehem or of the Child of Nazareth had it not been for the watchful care and faithful service of Joseph.

Photo, Three Lions, Inc.

HOLY FAMILY, Titian

Joseph

How weary and how tired they must have been,
Coming from Nazareth since the day's pale start,
Joseph with great responsibility,
Mary bearing earth's Savior neath her heart.
Nearing the village at the set of sun,
The man must hasten for a place to rest;
He watched the woman with grave, anxious eyes,
Seeing her clutch a white hand to her breast.

Was she too tired? Had they come too far?
Had his love failed this gentle, precious one?
And now the crowded inn, the words ''No room''
For Mary soon to mother God's dear Son!
Joseph was deeply troubled. Could there be
No place in all this throng for them to go?
Then, suddenly, the stable and a hand
Bidding them enter. God had planned it so!

Grace Noll Crowell

17

For Our Children

Lord Jesus, who didst take little children into Thine arms and laugh and play with them, bless, we pray Thee, all children at this Christmastide. As with shining eyes and glad hearts they nod their heads so wisely at the stories of the angels, and of a baby cradled in the hay at the end of the way of a wandering star, may their faith and expectation be a rebuke to our own faithlessness.

Help us to make this season all joy for them, a time that shall make Thee, Lord Jesus, even more real to them. Watch tenderly over them and keep them safe. Grant that they may grow in health and strength into Christian maturity. May they turn early to Thee, the Friend of children, the Friend of all. We ask in the lovely name of Him who was once a little child. Amen.

Peter Marshall

Before the paling of the stars,
  Before the winter morn,
  Before the earliest cockcrow,
  Jesus Christ was born;
    Born in a stable,
  Cradled in a manger,
In the world His hands had made,
  Born a stranger.

Priest and king lay fast asleep
  In Jerusalem,
Young and old lay fast asleep
  In crowded Bethlehem;
Saint and angel, ox and ass,
  Kept a watch together,
  Before the Christmas daybreak
  In the winter weather.

Jesus on His Mother's breast,
  In the stable cold,
Spotless Lamb of God was He,
  Shepherd of the fold:
Let us kneel with Mary Maid,
  With Joseph bent and hoary,
With saint and angel, ox and ass,
  To hail the King of glory.

Christina Rossetti

A Christmas Carol

19

"Elisabeth was filled with the Holy Spirit and said, Blessed art thou among women" (Luke 1:41-42).

Mary, Blessed Among Women

"The virgin's name was Mary." So Luke introduces the mother of Jesus. She is presented as the young virgin of Nazareth who was engaged to marry Joseph, of the house and lineage of David and a carpenter in the village. Luke has already told us that six months before this, the angel Gabriel had appeared to Zacharias in Jerusalem and announced that his wife Elisabeth would bear a son to be called John. Now the angel Gabriel comes to Mary in her humble home with his momentous tidings. The angel thus salutes Mary, "Hail, thou that art highly favored, the Lord is with thee." He then quiets her troubled mind by saying, "Fear not, Mary, for thou has found favor with God." And he then reveals to her the wonderful mystery that she is to become the mother of Jesus, the Son of the Most High.

To whom shall we go for an authentic word concerning the miracle of Christmas? Who will speak to us, and who will reveal to us the mystery of the lowly birth of the Son of the Most High? There are many voices to be heard: the voices of prophets and priests, of angels, shepherds, saints and Wise Men. There are the voices of a pagan emperor and a wicked Judean king, of terrified children and weeping mothers. But there is also the voice of the virgin whose pure heart first carried the secret of the Messiah's birth. Of all these voices, do we not prefer to listen to that of the mother of our Savior as she speaks of the deep things within her soul?

But we know Mary is not given to much speaking. We think of her as a quiet, gentle, reticent woman; she is thoughtful, meditative and reserved. She has a profound capacity for spiritual exultation and, when the occasion arises, has a remarkable gift for expressing her feelings in beautiful language. But her foremost characteristic is her meditative reserve, emphatically suggested by the statement, "But Mary kept all these sayings, pondering them in her heart."

When Mary does speak, she has something important to say. It is interesting to observe that the Nativity records contain just three instances of Mary's speaking. What she said in two of these cases is of paramount importance to a right understanding of the meaning of Christmas.

Painting opposite:
THE VISITATION
Carl Heinrich Bloch
(Photo, Three Lions, Inc.)

Mary's first utterance recorded in the pages of Luke is a question. It is the momentous hour, the sacred occasion of the Annunciation. The angel Gabriel has suddenly intruded upon her quiet homelife in Nazareth with the salutation: "Hail, thou that art highly favored, the Lord is with thee . . . Fear not, Mary, for thou hast found favor with God." He then delivers his message "And behold, thou shalt conceive in thy womb, and bring forth a son, and shalt call his name Jesus. He shall be great, and shall be called the Son of the Highest; and the Lord God shall give unto him the throne of his father David: and he shall reign over the house of Jacob for ever; and of his kingdom there shall be no end."

"And Mary said unto the angel, How shall this be, seeing I know not a man?"

It is clear that Mary does not doubt the promise. A simple question is all that comes from her. Her great strength of character and purity of faith are revealed in the simplicity of her brief but direct question. She asks only for information. Her words may be paraphrased as, "I believe what thou hast said to be true; but I do not understand how it will come to pass." Mary does not suppose for a moment that the promised child is to be the child of Joseph. So it is natural that she should want to know by what mysterious means God would give the promised son. Mary's question is in reality a confession of her faith in God's power to accomplish the supernatural in and through her.

That Mary's question was so regarded as a confession of faith and as a positive affirmation concerning the promised fact is seen in the angel's response. He does not rebuke Mary as he had rebuked Zacharias. He readily accepts her request for further information and fully discloses the mystery to her. "And the angel answered and said unto her, the Holy Spirit shall come upon thee, and the power of the Highest shall overshadow thee: therefore also that holy thing which shall be born of thee shall be called the Son of God."

The angel Gabriel has delivered God's message, unfolding the Divine plan and purpose. He has revealed the beautiful mystery of the miraculous conception; he has described the character and mission of the Son of the Most High; and he has graciously revealed to Mary the sign concerning her kinswoman, Elisabeth. Now the angel waits a moment, waiting for Mary's answer. He has spoken concerning God's wondrous and loving plan. The fulfillment of God's plan now waits upon her consent. What will Mary's answer be?

"And Mary said, Behold, the handmaid of the Lord; be it unto me according to thy word." Her reply is unsurpassed in all history as an expression of perfect faith. She confesses her implicit trust in the word from God and yields herself in complete submission to the will of God. There is no shrinking from all that the fulfillment of this promise might involve of suspicion, shame, reproach and suffering. Blessed indeed is Mary for the whole-hearted giving of herself to be used for the accomplishment of God's purposes. And blessed are all those who join with the virgin Mary through their surrender and obedience to the will of God.

A Christmas Carol

The Christ Child lay on Mary's lap,
His hair was like a light.
(O weary, weary were the world,
But here is all aright.)

The Christ Child lay on Mary's breast,
His hair was like a star.
(O stern and cunning are the kings,
But here the true hearts are.)

The Christ Child lay on Mary's heart,
His hair was like a fire.
(O weary, weary is the world,
But here the world's desire.)

The Christ Child stood at Mary's knee,
His hair was like a crown,
And all the flowers looked up at Him
And all the stars looked down.

G. K. Chesterton

One Small Child

One little child . . . no more, no less —
And could His mother Mary guess
Salvation for the human race
Depended on that night, that place?
And did she know this child would cause
All heaven to rock with glad applause?

Would cause the angels to rehearse
Their midnight song of sacred verse?
Would cause a star of strange design
To leave its orbit, and to shine

A brilliant path, from east to west?
Would cause wise men to choose the best
Of hoarded treasure, and to search
The nations from a camel perch?

Would make a king (in craven fear)
Destroy small man-children near?
To this small child the nation thrilled,
For He was prophecy fulfilled.

But could His mother, even, guess
While rocking Him with tenderness
The whole import of His advent,
This one small child — from heaven sent.

Esther S. Buckwalter

The Twelfth Christmas

Softly the twilight had fallen,
The stars appeared one by one,
While on a carpenter's doorstep
Sat a mother and her son.
Her mind was filled with memories
As she watched the fading light;
Many mysteries in her life
Were casting shadows tonight.

A sense of foreboding disturbed her
As she drew the boy to her side.
"My son, I wish you could always
In safety with me abide."
"But Mother, hast thou forgotten
That this is the day of days?
I am growing to be a man,
And will care for thee always."

"Nay, my son, I did not forget;
But today I have been sad.
I have no birthday gift for thee,
And I want thee to be glad."
"Tell me of the three caskets,
As today I am twelve years old
And thou hast promised, Mother dear,
To tell me of things yet untold."

"All day I thought of the caskets;
I know they mean much to me,
But thou has never opened them
That the contents I may see.
Always when I ask about them,
I am told that I must wait
Until able to understand,
For they are rare gifts of state."

Twelve wonderful years of his life
His mother had kept him her own,
Hiding the mystery in her heart,
His mission as she had known.
But tonight, her heart understood;
Sands of time had quickly run;
For now she must give back to God
This wonderful gift — his Son.

"Stay thou near me, my little son,
For when I hold thee fast
And know thou dost belong to God,
We have riches that will last.
I've treasured all these memories,
I will tell them now to thee
Because I know the time is here,
God's plan thou must clearly see.

"There were shepherds watching their flocks,
Who saw the heavens aflame,
And while this bright light was shining
An angel from heaven came.

'Fear not,' he said to the shepherds,
'For I bring tidings of peace;
A Savior born in Bethlehem
From sin the world will release.

" 'Follow the light to the manger,
This shall be to thee a sign:
The babe is wrapped in swaddling clothes,
But He is the King, Divine.'
Then came the angels from heaven
Singing of peace and great joy;
For God had sent his Son on earth
In the form of a baby boy.

"Then from the east came the wise men,
They had traveled from afar,
God guided them all the journey
By a bright and gleaming star.
And it led them to the manger
Where its glory filled the place.

"They were men of wealth and prestige,
But they worshiped at thy shrine
And laid at thy feet costly gifts,
For they knew thou wert divine.
These gifts were the lovely caskets,
The gold, frankincense and myrrh.

"Frankincense for worship given,
Power symbolized in gold —
Would that we could forget the third,
Think only of what I've told;
For the sad message of the myrrh
Since then has clouded my life;
I know fulfilling thy mission,
Death enters into the strife.

"But always we must remember
Thou art God's begotten son,
A gift in mystery given
That His kingdom here might come."
"It is a strange story, Mother,
But I know that it is true;
God has sent me into the world
That I his great work may do.

"I must do my Father's bidding;
Today I am twelve years old,
And He will make it plain to me,
So his plan I can unfold.
I will give the world his message,
That all men may understand
That I have come from the Father
To reveal his love for man.

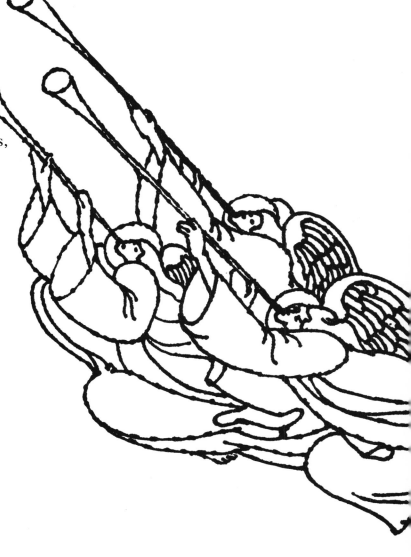

"Thou art blessed among all women
In giving this world God's gift;
I will be true to my mission,
Burdens from others will lift.
The hour is growing late, Mother,
And now thou must seek thy rest.
May I thank thee for the story,
It's a birthday gift — the best."

The lad alone on the doorstep,
Awaiting the cool, gray dawn;
In his heart he heard the angels
Singing their marvelous song.
And his Father's voice from heaven
Borne to him by the breeze:
"Thou art my own beloved son,
In Thee I am well pleased."

Ona Jane Meens

"But Mary kept all these sayings, pondering them in her heart" (Luke 2:19).

The Pondering Heart

At the time of Jesus' birth, the little town of Bethlehem was crowded with visitors and filled with confusion and excitement. It was like a great homecoming for those who belonged to the house and family of King David. The matter of their lodging being cared for, the visitors could give themselves over to the pleasures and opportunities of the occasion. They could meet and mingle with old friends and acquaintances, spend the time of their brief sojourn in discussing the news of the day and recall memories of past good times together. It was a glad, gay, busy and carefree occasion such as most holidays afford.

Only a few immediate relatives and close friends paid any attention to the distress of Mary and Joseph. When Mary's child was born, the news quickly spread throughout the village. The women all knew it first and told their husbands; but the busy crowds of visitors gave it little thought. *"Did you hear that a poor peasant woman from Nazareth gave birth to a son last night?" "Yes, and what a pity she had to go through such an ordeal at this time and in such a place!" "Why, they say that she had to dress the baby with her own hands, and lay him in a manger!"* An interesting item of news, a bit unusual to be sure, but for most of the visitors, just a means of passing the day. When they went back to their homes after completing the business of enrollment, they remained in complete ignorance of the meaning of the event that had come to pass in Bethlehem while they were there. Although it was the greatest event of all time, those who were closest to it knew nothing of its meaning!

There were a few, however, who gained impressions which remained with them all their lives. Some shepherds came in from nearby fields with a wonderful story to tell. They found Mary and Joseph and the baby, lying in the manger, and related what the angel had said to them concerning this child. "And the shepherds returned, glorifying and praising God for all the things that they had heard and seen, even as it was spoken unto them." Of course, they never forgot the experience of that wonderful night when the angels of heaven spoke good tidings to them and sang their hymn of glory and of peace.

The shepherds repeated again and again the saying of the angel. The people who heard their story were filled with wonder and astonishment. "But Mary kept all these sayings, pondering them in her heart." She was neither surprised nor astonished as were the inhabitants of Bethlehem. She and Joseph had both been prepared for these miraculous events by the revelations of the angels. Mary did not tell her experiences at this time but kept them quietly in her heart.

We may be assured that the Christmas treasures we keep will belong to the heart and the spirit. In Mary's experience, the angels went away again into heaven; the shepherds withdrew and went back to their sheepfolds; the Wise Men presented their costly gifts and departed. The swiftly moving scenes of new lands and peoples passed before her eyes, but the wonderful revelations concerning the Savior were treasured in her mother's heart forever. It is a very strange thing that, as far as we know, Jesus never returned to Bethlehem, the scene of his birth. But we may be sure that Mary made many a pilgrimage in memory to the place where she laid her firstborn Son in the lowly manger.

The way of the pondering heart is our road to Bethlehem. We may go there in our thoughts as we meditate upon the story of Christmas. Like the shepherds of old, we must resolve to make this pilgrimage. It requires an act of will and determination on our part. "Let us now go even unto Bethlehem." Many will not go; they will be too busy with the outward paraphernalia of Christmas. But we must determine to go; we must go now, before it is too late. It is not an easy matter to go; we must take time; we must make sacrifices; we must put aside pressing matters. But we must go, even though the way be difficult, if we are to find the Christ and the new life he has for us.

Paradox

Here lies the precious Babe, first-fruit of virgin's womb,
Angels' delight and joy, men's highest price and boon,
Should He your Savior be and lift you into God,
Then, man, stay near the crib and make it your abode.

> How simple we must grow!
> How simple they, who came!
> The shepherds looked at God
> Long before any man.
> He sees God nevermore
> Not there, nor here on earth
> Who does not long within
> To be a shepherd first.

All things are now reversed: the castle's in the cave,
The crib becomes the throne, the night brings forth the day,
The virgin bears a child; O man! reflect and say
That heart and mind must be reversed in every way.

Angelus Silesius

31

ADORATION OF THE CHILD, Gerard von Honthorst

Only an Hour

For an hour on Christmas Eve
And again on the holy day
Seek the magic of past time,
From this present turn away.
Dark though our day,
Light is the snow on the hawthorn bush
And the ox knelt down at midnight.

Only an hour, only an hour
From wars and confusions turn away
To the islands of old time
When the world was simple and gay,
Or so we say,
And light lay the snow on the green holly,
The tall oxen knelt at midnight.

Caesar and Herod shared the world,
Sorrow over Bethlehem lay,
Iron the empire, brutal the time,
Dark was the day,
Light lay the snow on the mistletoe berries
And the ox knelt down at midnight.

Robinson Jeffers

The Shepherd
Who Stayed
Behind

The shepherds were watching their flocks one night,
    And the stillness was deep and clear;
When an angel appeared in the sky above,
    And the shepherds were filled with fear,
"Lo," said the angel, "I bring you good news,
    A Savior this day has been born;
A sign I will give you to show you the way
    To the stable He now adorns."

Then suddenly the night filled with music and song
    And praises to God up above;
That peace and goodwill might reign thus supreme
    Through Jesus, the gift of God's love.
Then quickly the angels were gone away,
    And the stillness was deep and bright;
But the shepherds were never the same again
    As they were on that fateful night.

Then when they were able to speak once more,
    They questioned just what they should do;
When someone suggested they follow the star
    To see if the angel spoke true.
And there in the manger they found the Babe
    As the angel did prophesy;
Then returned to the fields from whence they had come
    To honor and glorify.

Now the lot fell to one that he stay behind
    And guard every sheep in the field;
While others might journey to search for the truth,
    This pleasure he found he must yield.
And when in the still and the deep of the night
    He dwelt on the things he had seen,
He wondered and marveled that such could be true,
    That a babe had been sent to be King.

And he questioned how one of such lowly birth
    Could now change a world steeped in sin;
Or give life eternal to those who believed
    That He was the Savior of men.
But had not the prophet Isaiah foretold
    The coming of just such a one,
Some hundreds of years long before this night,
    And He would be God's only Son?

Thus reasoned the shepherd that most holy night
    And knew that the story was true;
Then felt his heart quicken with warmth and delight
    And faith that was suddenly new.
Awareness, as never before was now his,
    And he cherished each moment with bliss;
The others had traveled to search out the truth,
    But the truth he now knew was just this:

That faith is believing in things unseen,
    Not asking for proof that it's so;
Not asking to touch, or to see, or to hear,
    Just trusting what somehow one knows.
And strangely the shepherd now knew without doubt
    That the great Prince of Peace had been born;
That he must acclaim Him as Savior of men,
    Let others give vent to their scorn.

The dawn was a matter of moments away,
    When the shepherds returned with their news;
But the radiant look on the watchman's face
    Only caused them to be more confused.
And even their flocks seemed to sense this great change,
    As if somehow they too were aware
That a visit by angels had favored a few;
    A privilege they also had shared.

And now it is Christmas on earth once again,
    But the story is just as new;
Except that it's told for all who believe,
    And not for a privileged few.
And if, like the shepherd, you know beyond doubt,
    That God gave his Son as a gift;
What less should we offer than SELF in return,
    To be used as the Father sees fit?

Chleo Deshler Goodman

35

"Let us now go even unto Bethlehem" (Luke 2:15).

Roads to Bethlehem

With the coming of Advent Sunday, the minds and hearts of the people of Christendom will be directed, for a few weeks, toward Bethlehem. It will become, for a time at least, the spiritual capital of the world—not the capitals of the great nations, but "thou Bethlehem, in the land of Judah." Pilgrimages will be made to Bethlehem; throngs of people will go to the place where Jesus was born; millions more will make the pilgrimage spiritually, in thought, imagination, desire and aspiration.

In view of this universal desire for a pilgrimage, it seems good to explore the roads that lead to Bethlehem. First, the roads that led to Bethlehem when Jesus was born; secondly, the roads we must travel as spiritual pilgrims if we are to rediscover the realities of Bethlehem.

First, there is the providential road. This was the road Mary and Joseph traveled. On the surface, the record seems to contradict this. The record speaks of another power that compelled Joseph and Mary to make the journey to Bethlehem. "In those days a decree went out from Caesar Augustus that all the world should be enrolled." It appears to be the power of the state; the Roman Empire, the decree of Caesar, lord of the world, that compelled Joseph and Mary to make the journey at this inopportune time.

The journey was difficult and hazardous for the pair. They traveled the hundred miles or more by foot and by donkey. Especially for Mary did the journey involve physical discomfort and distress. No doubt both suffered mental anguish as to what might happen to Mary's unborn child. The hardships of the journey from Nazareth to the city of David were accentuated by the reception that awaited them at Bethlehem. For these weary visitors, there was "no room in the inn." The only refuge they could find was in the stable at the rear of the courtyard of the inn. So much for the human side of the story.

This was indeed a providential journey, not only for Joseph and Mary, but also for the whole world. Joseph and Mary went to Bethlehem because they were of the house and lineage of David. It was God's age-long providential plan that selected Mary as the mother of Jesus, the promised Messiah. It was God's age-long plan that the Son of David, as the Messiah was called, should be born in Bethlehem, the City of David. This event was prophesied by Micah:

> And thou Bethlehem, in the land of Judah, art not the least among
> the princes of Judah: for out of thee shall come forth a Governor,
> that shall rule my people Israel (Matt. 2:6).

It was God's age-long, providential plan that His only begotten Son should be cradled in the manger of Bethlehem. Who but God could have thought of giving his Son to the world in this lowly, divinely human manner.

Second, there is the glory road. This was the road the shepherds traveled. In Luke's account of the birth of Jesus, the story of what the shepherds saw and heard and found and reported makes up the greater portion of the record. These shepherds were watching their flocks in the fields not far from Bethlehem. Suddenly an angel of the Lord appeared to them, and the glory of the Lord shone round about them. The herald angel proclaimed to them the good tidings of the Savior's birth and revealed to them the sign by which they should find and know the newborn King. Whereupon a multitude of angels joined the herald angel, praising God with their song of glory and of peace.

The shepherds received this glorious revelation with awe and wonder and believed the message in their hearts. They accepted it as something the Lord had made known to them; and they resolved to act at once upon the heavenly mandate that had been laid upon them. "The shepherds said one to another, Let us now go even unto Bethlehem, and see this thing that is come to pass." They lost no time in verifying the word of the angel concerning the Christmas miracle, the Babe of Bethlehem. "And they came with haste and found both Mary and Joseph, and the babe lying in the manger." Thus the humble shepherds were privileged to behold the sweetest, most tender and holy sight ever granted to mortals: the sight of the little Lord Jesus cradled in his manger bed. Aside from Mary and Joseph, the shepherds were the first to see the newborn Savior of the world.

Surely it was a glory road the shepherds traveled from the outlying plains to the manger where the infant Savior lay! The glory of the Lord shone upon that road, and the message and the music of the angels of heaven lighted up the path they took in eager haste to find the Babe of Bethlehem. Likewise, their return journey was a glory road, too. For "the shepherds returned, glorifying and praising God for all they had heard and seen, even as it was spoken unto them." We may be certain that they traveled this glory road in the years ahead, and that they helped others to find it by their faithful witness and testimony to the wonderful things they had heard and seen.

O strange indifference! low and high
Drowsed over common joys and cares:
The earth was still — but knew not why;
The world was listening — unawares;
How calm a moment may precede
One that shall thrill the world forever!
To that still moment none would heed,
Man's doom was linked no more to sever,
In the solemn midnight
Centuries ago.

It is the calm and solemn night!
A thousand bells ring out and throw
Their joyous peals abroad, and smile
The darkness, charmed and holy now!
The night that erst no name had worn,
To it a happy name is given;
For in that stable lay newborn
The peaceful Prince of Earth and Heaven,
In the solemn midnight
Centuries ago.

Alfred Domett

O Strange
Indifference!

39

ADORATION OF THE SHEPHERDS, Christian Dietrich

A Hymn
on the Nativity
of My Savior

I sing the birth was born tonight,
The Author both of life and light;
The angels so did sound it,
And like the ravished shepherds said,
Who saw the light and were afraid,
Yet searched, and true they found it.

The Son of God, th' Eternal King,
That did us all salvation bring
And freed the soul from danger;
He whom the whole world could not take,
The Word which heaven and earth did make,
Was now laid in a manger.

Ben Jonson

41

Third, there is the star-lit road. This was the road the Wise Men traveled. When they first saw the star in the night sky, they undertook the long and difficult journey from Ecbatana in Persia, to Jerusalem in Judea. This was a journey of more than a thousand miles and required from three to six months by camel train. They had to travel over the Zagros mountains of Persia, through the valleys of the Tigris and Euphrates rivers of Babylonia, across the vast stretches of the Syrian desert. Costly equipment and provisions would be necessary. They must endure perils of robbers, wild beasts, storms, floods and desert wastes. But they traveled this long and dangerous road to Judea, because the light of the star shone upon them.

When they arrived at Jerusalem, they faced new difficulties. Their question, "Where is he that is born King of the Jews?" disturbed and troubled Herod and all Jerusalem. They were delayed by Herod's inquiry of the priests and scribes as to where the Christ should be born. They were further delayed and distressed by being summoned to a private audience with the crafty and malicious king who ordered them to do what their conscience could not permit them to do. But, finally, they were permitted to continue their journey to Bethlehem.

Was there ever such a journey as this? As they left the city at nightfall, the star once more appeared and went before them all the way to Bethlehem. Their hearts were filled with joy as they followed the star-lit road which led them to the very place where the Christ Child was. "And they came into the house and saw the young child with Mary his mother; and they fell down and worshiped him; and opening their treasures, they offered unto him gifts of gold and frankincense and myrrh." The star-lit road they had followed all the way brought them at last to Him who was the Bright and Morning Star, the Sun of Righteousness, the Light of the World.

The Wise Men did not just happen to come to Bethlehem; they did not just stumble upon the treasure hidden in the Judean field. Rather their discovery was the culmination and reward of their lifelong quest for light and truth and salvation. They were not unlike the merchant who made it his business to seek goodly pearls and who, when he found one pearl of surpassing beauty and worth, sold all his other pearls that he might buy this one pearl of great price. So we must recognize in Christ the supreme treasure of life, of time and eternity, and we must be willing to count all other things as loss, that we may gain Christ and be found in Him.

All of these roads to Bethlehem stretch before us: the providential road, the glory road, the star-lit road. Let us nobly resolve, as did the shepherds: "Let us now go even unto Bethlehem."

A
Nativity
Song

How far is it to Bethlehem?
  Not very far.
Shall we find the stable room
  Lit by a star?

Can we see the little Child,
  Is He within?
If we lift the wooden latch
  May we go in?

May we stroke the creatures there,
  Ox, ass, or sheep?
May we peep like them and see
  Jesus asleep?

If we touch His tiny hand
  Will He awake?
Will He know we've come so far
  Just for His sake?

Great kings have precious gifts
  And we have naught,
Little smiles and little tears
  Are all we brought.

For all weary children
  Mary must weep,
Here, on His bed of straw,
  Sleep, children, sleep.

God in His mother's arms,
  Babes in the byre,
Sleep, as they sleep who find
  Their heart's desire.

Frances Chesterton

Photo, Three Lions, Inc.

THE JOURNEY OF THE MAGI, Stefano Sassetta

Star of the Nativity

It was wintertime.
The wind was blowing from the plains.
And the infant was cold in the cave
On the slope of a hill.

He was warmed by the breath of an ox.
Every farmyard beast
Huddled safe in the cave;
A warm mist drifted over the manger.

On a rock afar some drowsy shepherds
Shook off the wisps of straw
And hayseed of their beds,
And sleepily gazed into the vast of night.

They saw gravestones, fences, fields,
The shafts of a cart
Deep in drifted snows,
And a sky of stars above the graveyard.

And, shyer than a watchman's light,
One star alone
Unseen until then
Shone bright on the way to Bethlehem.

At times it rose, a haystack aflame,
Apart from God and the sky,
Like a barn set on fire,
Like a farmstead ablaze in the night.

It reared in the sky like a flaming stack
Of thatch and hay,
In the midst of Creation
Surprised by this new star in the world.

The flame grew steadily deeper, wider,
Large as a portent.
Three stargazers then
Hastened to follow this marvelous light.

Behind them, their camels with gifts;
Their caparisoned asses, each one smaller
In size, came daintily down the hillside.

And all new matters of ages to come
Arose as a vision of wonder in space.
All thoughts of ages, all dreams, new worlds,
All the future of galleries and of museums,
All the games of fairies, the work of inventors,
The yule trees, and the dreams of all children dream,
The tremulous glow of candles in rows,
The gold and silver of angels and globes
(A wind blew, raging, long from the plain)
And the splendor of tinsel and toys under trees.

A part of the pond lay hidden by alders;
A part could be seen afar from the cliff
Where rooks were nesting among the treetops.
The shepherds could see each ass and camel
Trudging its way by the water mill.
"Let us go and worship the miracle,"
They said, and belted their sheepskin coats.

Their bodies grew warm, walking through snows.
There were footprints that glinted like mica
Across bright fields, on the way to the inn.
But the dogs on seeing the tracks in starshine
Growled loud in anger, as if at a flame.

The frosty night was like a fairy tale.
And phantoms from mountain ridges in snows
Invisibly came to walk in the crowd.
The dogs grew fearful of ghosts around
And huddled beside the shepherd lads.

Across these valleys and mountain roads,
Unbodied, unseen by mortal eyes,
A heavenly host appeared in the throng,
And each footprint gleamed as an angel's foot.

At dawn the cedars lifted their heads.
A multitude clustered around the cave.
"Who are you?" said Mary. They spoke: "We come
As shepherds of flocks, as envoys of heaven:
In praise of the Child and your glory we come."
"There's no room in the cave; you must wait outside."

Before dawnlight, in gloom, in ashen dark,
The drivers and shepherds stamped in the cold.
The footmen quarreled with mounted men;
Near the well and the wooden water trough
The asses brayed and the camels bellowed.
The dawn! It swept the last of the stars
Like flecks of ash from the vaulted sky.

Then Mary allowed the Magi alone
To enter the cleft of the mountainside.
He slept in His manger in radiant light,
As a moonbeam sleeps in a hollow tree.
The breath of the ox and the ass kept warm
His hands and feet in the cold of night.

The Magi remained in the twilight cave;
They whispered softly, groping for words.
Then someone in darkness touched the arm
Of one near the manger, to move him aside:
Behold, like a guest above the threshold,
The Star of the Nativity gazed on the Virgin.

Boris Pasternak,
translated by Eugene M. Kayden

There's
a Song
in the Air!

There's a song in the air!
There's a star in the sky!
There's a mother's deep prayer
And a baby's low cry!
And the star rains its fire
While the beautiful sing,
For the manger of Bethlehem cradles a King!

There's a tumult of joy
O'er the wonderful birth,
For the Virgin's sweet Boy
Is the Lord of the earth.
Ay! the star rains its fire
While the beautiful sing,
For the manger of Bethlehem cradles a King!

We rejoice in the light,
And we echo the song
That comes down through the night
From the heavenly throng.
Ay! we shout to the lovely evangel they bring,
And we greet in his cradle our Savior and King!

Josiah Gilbert Holland

Photo, Three Lions, Inc.

The Glorious Revelation

On the night of Christ's Nativity, the shepherds went to their fields and flocks just as on previous nights. They did not expect anything unusual to happen to affect them beyond the ordinary demands and duties of their work. It could be that the stars shone brighter that night; perhaps the clear air was vibrant with suppressed voices; maybe the winds stirred the branches softly like the rustle of angels' wings. Certainly the shepherds were totally unprepared for what was about to happen.

On that night, God was watching the shepherds, even as they were watching their sheep. The hour had come for the curtain to be lifted. An angel appeared to the shepherds and the glory of the Lord was revealed. The angel delivered his message and withdrew, but a great multitude then sang from the portals of heaven, proclaiming their majestic hymn of glory and peace. Then the curtain again fell.

This revelation was granted to the shepherds without any effort on their part. They remained where they were, engaged in their ordinary tasks exactly as they had been on many nights previous. They were in their own fields and familiar surroundings when the glory of the Lord broke upon them. The shepherds were not searching for angels, but only shepherding sheep; the angels sought out the shepherds.

This revelation granted to the shepherds was clear, definite and complete. The messenger told them who was born: "A Savior, Christ the Lord." He told them where to find him: "in the city of David." He told them when to find him: "this day;" and he told them how to know him: "ye shall find a babe wrapped in swaddling clothes, and lying in a manger." The shepherds were also told why the Savior was born, that "good tidings of great joy might come "to all the people." The song of the heavenly choir revealed to the shepherds the ultimate purpose behind all, namely, that "glory to God in the highest" might result and "peace among men" on earth might prevail. What more did the shepherds need to know? They had received all the information needed. God's revelations, instructions and directions are always clear enough and definite enough for faith, obedience and action. The shepherds accepted and acted upon the knowledge they had, and God led them forward.

Thus, while we give glory to God for his gracious revelation to the shepherds, we must not fail to note the special fitness of the shepherds in being thus chosen and honored. These men were evidently prepared in heart and spirit to be faithful recipients and witnesses of the tidings of the Savior's birth. James Stalker, in "The Life of Christ," tells why the angels came to the shepherds with their heavenly message. "And seeking the most worthy hearts to which they might communicate it, they found them in these simple shepherds living the life of contemplation and prayer in the same fields where Jacob had kept his flocks, where Boaz and Ruth had been wedded, and where David had spent his youth. There, by the study of the secrets and needs of their own hearts, learning far more of the nature of the Savior who was to come than the Pharisee amid the religious pomp of the temple or the scribe burrowing, without the seeing eye, among the prophecies of the Old Testament."

Hugh Thompson Kerr in "Old Things New" retells an incident from Bernard Shaw's *Saint Joan*. Following the coronation of King Charles of France, Joan tells the king and the archbishop that the heavenly voices are bidding her lead the armies of France on to victory; and she is sure that if only the king will not falter, success will come. But the king, impatient and worldly, replied, "Oh, your voices; your voices. Why don't the voices come to me? I am the king, not you." And Joan answered, "They do come to you, but you do not hear them. You have not sat in the field in the evening and listened for them. When the Angelus rings, you cross yourself and have done with it; but if you prayed from your heart and listened to the thrilling of the bells in the air after they had stopped ringing, you would hear voices as well as I do."

The shepherds were the first to receive the angelic tidings of the Savior's birth, yet another distinction belongs to them. They were also the first witnesses of the Christmas gospel; the first to tell others the good tidings of joy they had received. Faithfully, honestly, truthfully the shepherds told the story even as it had been given unto them. Their message was simple and complete. They were true witnesses; the only kind God can use as his spokesmen. They knew that the Lord had given them their message, and they were moved by divine inspiration to declare it to others. Theirs was the heaven-born integrity and compulsion that marked the witnessing of Peter and John when they declared, "we cannot but speak the things which we saw and heard." The message of the shepherds produced wonderment in the hearts of all who heard. There were evidently a number of folk in and around Bethlehem who heard what the shepherds had to tell; for the record reads, "And all that heard it wondered."

"And when they were come into the house, they saw the young child with Mary his mother, and fell down, and worshiped him; and when they had opened their treasures, they presented unto him gifts; gold, and frankincense, and myrrh" (Matt. 2:11).

How the Wise Men Found the Christ Child

The way of the Wise Men is the road to Bethlehem that most people follow. But who were these men from the east? They were undoubtedly Persian priests, Magi, wise men, seers of their land and time. They were star men, followers of Zoroaster, worshipers of light, students of astrology and astronomy. Their contemplation of the heavens stirred their deepest religious feelings and they regarded the stars as "the thoughts of the Eternal."

What were these learned men seeking? They were seeking what every aspiring human heart seeks, namely communion and fellowship with God. The words of St. Augustine apply to such questing spirits in all lands and generations: "Thou has made us for Thyself, O God, and our hearts are restless until they rest in Thee." These Wise Men of the east knew Hebrew scripture. They were familiar with the prophecy concerning the star out of Jacob; they shared and represented the wistful longing of the Gentile world for a brighter day. Nearly four hundred years before the birth of Christ, at the very height of Greek philosophy, art and drama Socrates said "We must wait until someone comes from God to instruct us how to behave toward the divinity and toward men." And Plato declared, "It is necessary that a law giver be sent from heaven to instruct us. Oh, how greatly do I desire to see that man and to know who he is." According to the Hebrew prophet, Isaiah, the ancient world was waiting and longing and searching for the Light of God! His prophetic declaration was, "And nations shall come to thy light, and kings to the brightness of thy rising."

How were these particular wise men specially prepared for the quest? We might say that their whole life was a spiritual pilgrimage. Through the highest medium that they knew, they were seeking for the true Light that lighteth every man. Hence, when his star appeared in the Orient sky, they were ready for the journey wherever it might lead.

When they finally arrived in Jerusalem, they were confronted with new difficulties. Their question, ''Where is he that is born King of the Jews?'' produced consternation, suspicion, and trouble, in that it aroused the envy of King Herod. Their urgent mission was delayed while Herod inquired of his chief priests and scribes where the Christ should be born. They were further delayed by the private audience with Herod who questioned them and commanded them to ''go and search out exactly concerning the young child; and when ye have found him, bring me word, that I also may come and worship him.''

When they finally resumed their journey toward Bethlehem, what a relief it must have been to leave the shadows of Herod's private domain and set forth on the star-lit road to Bethlehem. This was a quick, easy and happy journey of five or six miles that could be traveled in two or three hours.

And so the Wise Men came to Bethlehem. At this moment the Wise Men did two things ''they fell down and worshiped him; and [opening] their treasures [offered] unto him gifts, gold, and frankincense, and myrrh.'' How wise they were to worship and revere the child, Jesus, the Son of the Most High; they had found God, the Savior, the Light of the World in a child.

How laboriously you came,
taking sights and calculating
where the shepherds had run barefoot!
Yet you came,
and were not turned away.

For his sake
who did not reject
your curious gifts,
pray always for the learned,
the oblique,
the delicate.

Let them not be forgotten
at the Throne of God
when the simple
come into their Kingdom.

Evelyn Waugh

To the Three Kings

55

The Wise Men's Story

How shall we say if suddenly the sky
Was newly starred, or if our hearts were high
With visions of a destiny which led
Us on although we questioned where and why?

We followed love, and we were comforted
On that long journey by a light which fed
Our souls with faith which did not fade or die,
A light whose source lay on a manger bed.

We hoped to find a child but did not know
He would be in a stable, poor and small,
But filled with joy so great it seemed to flow
Like music, making every dream grow tall.

We are three kings who sought a palace door
But knelt, instead, to worship on a stable floor.

Lola S. Morgan

Photo, Three Lions, Inc.

THE ADORATION OF THE MAGI, Jean Bruegel

57

The Ballad of Befana

Befana the Housewife, scrubbing her pane,
Saw three old sages ride down the lane,
Saw three gray travelers pass her door —
Gaspar, Balthazar, Melchior.

"Where journey you, sirs?" she asked of them.
Balthazar answered, "To Bethlehem,

For we have news of a marvelous thing.
Born in a stable is Christ the King."

"Give Him my welcome!"
Then Gaspar smiled,
"Come with us, mistress, to greet the Child."

"Oh, happily, happily would I fare,
Were my dusting through and I'd polished the stair."

Old Melchior leaned on his saddle horn.
"Then send but a gift to the small Newborn."

"Oh, gladly, gladly I'd send Him one,
Were the hearthstone swept and my weaving done.

"As soon as ever I've baked my bread,
I'll fetch Him a pillow for His head,
And a coverlet too," Befana said.

"When the rooms are aired and the linen dry,
I'll look at the Babe."
But the Three rode by.

She worked for a day and a night and a day,
Then, gifts in her hands, took up her way.
But she never could find where the Christ Child lay.

And still she wanders at Christmastide,
Houseless, whose house was all her pride,

Whose heart was tardy, whose gifts were late;
Wanders, and knocks at every gate,
Crying, "Good people, the bells begin!
Put off your toiling and let love in."

Phyllis McGinley

58

Reprinted by permission of Curtis Brown, Ltd. Copyright © 1957 by Phyllis McGinley.

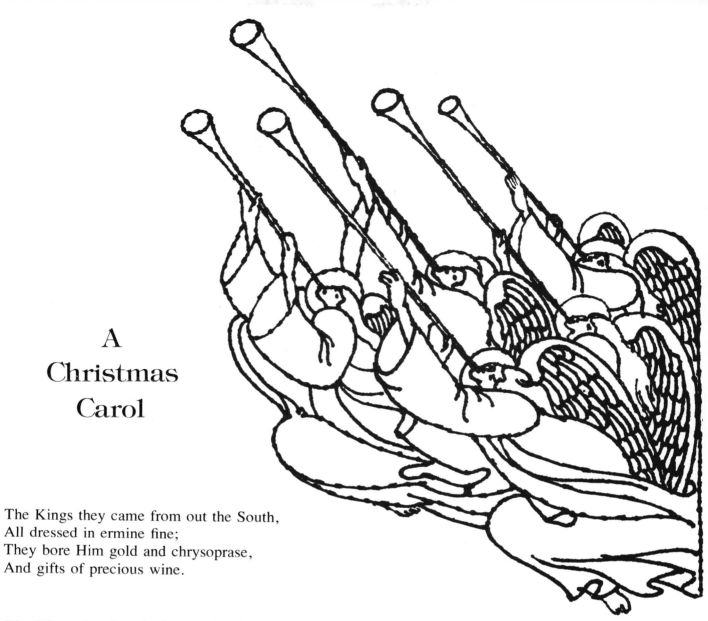

A Christmas Carol

The Kings they came from out the South,
All dressed in ermine fine;
They bore Him gold and chrysoprase,
And gifts of precious wine.

The Kings they knocked upon the door;
The Shepherds entered in;
The Wise Men followed after them,
To hear the song begin.

The Wise Men came from out the East,
And they were wrapped in white:
The star that led them all the way,
Did glorify the night.

The Shepherds came from out the North,
Their coats were brown and old;
They brought Him little new-born lambs —
They had not any gold.

The Angels came from heaven high,
And they were clad with wings;
And lo! they brought a joyful song
The host of heaven sings.

The Angels sang through all the night,
Until the rising sun,
But little Jesus fell asleep
Before the song was done.

Sara Teasdale

"And this shall be a sign unto you: Ye shall find the babe wrapped in swaddling clothes and lying in a manger" (Luke 2:12).

The Christmas Cradle

A careful reading of the familiar portions of the Gospel brings to light new truth and meaning. Most of us have read or heard read the Christmas story in Luke's Gospel scores of times. But have we ever observed how many times the manger is mentioned in the record? Luke mentions it three times and from three different points of view.

The first view of the manger sets forth the somber fact of man's rejections of the Messiah, foretold by the prophet Isaiah: "He is despised and rejected of men; a man of sorrows, and acquainted with grief . . . he was despised, and we esteemed him not" (53:3). The beginning of the fulfillment of this prophecy began at Jesus' birth when there was no room in the inn. Perhaps this rejection was unintentional and unavoidable. The innkeeper of Bethlehem did not know Mary and Joseph were coming; they had not made any room reservations in advance. The other visitors who crowded the little inn to capacity did not know about Mary and Joseph either. Some of them might have been kind enough to give up their rooms to Mary if they had known her desperate need.

The people did not know any better, but they should have known. They were simply too busy with their own affairs to be greatly concerned about the needs of others. Caesar was making his claims upon them and, as a result, God's claims were being overlooked. Today, also, too many lives are preoccupied with selfish aims, materialistic concerns, worldly pursuits which leave no room for God's plans and the interests of his Son.

The herald angel said to the shepherds, "And this is the sign unto you: Ye shall find a babe wrapped in swaddling clothes, and lying in a manger." We note that the word concerning the manger came to the shepherds as a revelation from heaven. The angel spoke of the manger cradle as a "sign"—a miracle of divine grace and power—so God must have planned it that way. It is strange and wonderful that the angel from heaven revealed the sign of the manger to lowly shepherds.

What does God say to humanity in the sign of the manger? Why does it hold such perennial fascination for the human heart? Why does it appeal to

Painting opposite:
THE NATIVITY
Il Baroccio
(Photo, Camera Clix)

61

young and old? The manger appeals to us because of its simplicity. We see a stable, a cattle stall, a manger; we see hay and straw and animals, all familiar, commonplace things.

The majestic lowliness of the manger also appeals to us. We know who this manger Child is: the King of Glory, Immanuel, the Son of the Most High, the Lord's High, the Lord's Christ, the world's Savior. Knowing this, we are awed by his condescension; his humiliation, his majestic lowliness. But most of all, the spiritual reality appeals to us. Why have the world's greatest artists lavished their skill and devotion upon this scene of the manger? Because of the spiritual truth, the eternal reality, the ennobling power of it. There is something about the manger scene that evokes the deepest feeling of the human soul.

Concerning the shepherds, it is said, "And they came with haste and found both Mary and Joseph, and the babe lying in the manger." The shepherds were the first to find the Savior in the manger. The reason they found him was that they were chosen to receive the good tidings of the Savior's birth. They believed and accepted the message as the word of the Lord. Moreover, they obeyed the mandate of the angel to go and seek him where he was to be found. Having done this, they discovered the family in the Bethlehem stable, and they worshiped the manger child as the savior and shepherd of his people. Their finding the Savior filled their hearts with the joy of salvation, and the truth they heard concerning him was to them the message of life.

We know what it meant to the shepherds of Bethlehem to find the Christ. What does it mean to those who find him today? For one thing, there

is the hope and promise of a better day in the newborn child. We know what the births of John the Baptist and of Jesus meant to the world. The birth of a child is still one of God's ways of saving the world and renewing the hopes of his people and advancing his kingdom.

In the year 1809, Napoleon's Austrian war seemed to hold the clue to the destiny of Europe and the world; but in the cradles of the world the future was being made. In that one year, William Gladstone was born at Liverpool, Alfred Tennyson at Somersby Rectory; Oliver Wendell Holmes in Massachusetts, Abraham Lincoln in Kentucky, Felix Mendelssohn at Hamburg. So also, while the world watched its Herods and Caesars, God's purpose for the future of mankind was cradled in the manger of Bethlehem. In our troubled day, we are anxiously watching the Caesars and the trend of political events. The evil cunning and wrath of Herod troubles all Jerusalem. But in the cradles of the world, in this very year, are being born the babies who in their appointed time will bring renewal and hope into the life of the world.

"Can any good thing come out of Nazareth?" is still a question that mocks human wisdom and foils the schemes of those who plot against the welfare of humanity. Out of obscure places like Bethlehem, God calls his servants to turn the tides of world history. So, after all, the future destiny of our nation and of the nations of the earth will not depend so much upon what comes out of Washington, or Moscow, or London, or Paris or Rome, but rather upon what comes from God's "Bethlehems" and the cradles of his anointed children of destiny. The manger of Bethlehem is still the hope of the world!

What could be done? The inn was full of folks!
His honor, Marcus Lucius, and his scribes
Who made the census: honorable men
From farthest Galilee, come hitherward
To be enrolled; high ladies and their lords;
The rich, the rabbis, such a noble throng
As Bethlehem had never seen before
And may not see again. And there they were,
Close-herded with their servants, till the inn
Was like a hive at swarming-time, and I
Was fairly crazed among them.

    Could I know
That they were so important? Just the two,
No servants, just a workman sort of man,
Leading a donkey, and his wife thereon
Drooping and pale . . . I saw them not myself,
My servants must have driven them away;
But had I seen them, how was I to know?
Were inns to welcome stragglers, up and down
In all our towns from Beersheba to Dan,
Till He should come? And how were men to know?

There was a sign, they say, a heavenly light
Resplendent: but I had no time for stars,
And there were songs of angels in the air
Out on the hills; but how was I to hear
Amid the thousand clamors of an inn?
Of course, if I had known them, who they were,
And who was He that should be born that night,
For now I learn that they will make him King,
A second David, who will ransom us
From these Philistine Romans . . . who but He
That feeds an army with a loaf of bread,
And if a soldier falls, He touches him
And up he leaps, uninjured? Had I known,
I would have turned the whole inn upside down,
His honor, Marcus Lucius, and the rest,
And sent them all to stables, had I known.

So you have seen Him, stranger, and perhaps
Again may see Him? Prithee say for me,
I did not know; and if He comes again
As He will surely come, with retinue,
And banners, and an army, tell my Lord
That all my inn is His to make amends.

Alas! Alas! to miss a chance like that!
This inn that might be chief among them all,
The birthplace of Messiah . . . had I known!

Amos Russell Wells

The Inn

The Landlord Speaks A.D. 28

Painting opposite:
NO ROOM AT THE INN
Robert Heuel

Photo, Three Lions, Inc.

ADORATION OF THE SHEPHERDS BY NIGHT, *Guido Reni*

Hay,
Did You Say?

Hay! hay did you say?
Surely it was not hay
On which the Christ Child lay?
Humble indeed the shed,
Awkward the manger bed,
Was there no linen spread?
Come, was it hay you said?

Yes, it was common hay,
Cut on a summer's day;
As the sweet crop they drest —
Dividing good from best —
They knew not some would rest
This world's most holy Guest.

Author Unknown

The House of Christmas

There fared a mother driven forth
Out of an inn to roam;
In the place where she was homeless
All men are at home.
The crazy stable close at hand,
With shaking timber and shifting sand,
Grew a stronger thing to abide and stand
Than the square stones of Rome.

For men are homesick in their homes,
And strangers under the sun,
And they lay their heads in a foreign land
Whenever the day is done.
Here we have battle and blazing eyes,
And chance and honour and high surprise,
But our homes are under miraculous skies
Where the yule tale was begun.

A Child in a foul stable,
Where the beasts feed and foam;
Only where He was homeless
Are you and I at home;
We have hands that fashion and heads that know,
But our hearts we lost—how long ago!
In a place no chart nor ship can show
Under the sky's dome.

This world is wild as an old wives' tale,
And strange the plain things are,
The earth is enough and the air is enough
For our wonder and our war;
But our rest is as far as the fire-drake swings
And our peace is put in impossible things
Where clashed and thundered unthinkable wings
Round an incredible star.

To an open house in the evening
Home shall men come,
To an older place than Eden
And a taller town than Rome.
To the end of the way of the wandering star,
To the things that cannot be and that are,
To the place where God was homeless
And all men are at home.

G. K. Chesterton

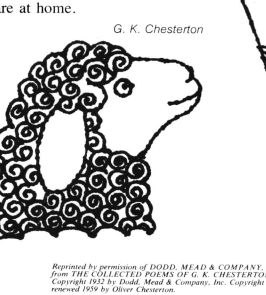

"Neither do men light a candle, and put it under a bushel, but on a candlestick; and it giveth light unto all that are in the house. Let your light so shine before men, that they may see your good works, and glorify your Father which is in heaven" (Matt. 5:15-16).

Wherever Christmas is truly experienced and kept, it will be in the hearts and homes and churches of those who have borrowed their light from the Christ Child; who have lighted their altar lamps of love, devotion and worship with the candles from Bethlehem. Let us consider some of these candles from Bethlehem which keep the light and warmth of Christmas aglow in countless human hearts.

Candle of Memory

First, there is the candle of hallowed memory. Bethlehem is mentioned in fourteen books of the Bible. It is first mentioned in Genesis as the place where Rachel died and was buried. Bethlehem was the home of Elimelech and his family before their ill-fated journey into the land of Moab. Here, the widowed Naomi returned with her daughter-in-law, Ruth the Moabitess; and here also Ruth gleaned in the barley fields of Boaz, the wealthy farmer of Bethlehem. Ruth and Boaz were married in Bethlehem, and their son Obed was born there. Bethlehem was the birthplace and ancestral home of David. In the neighboring fields, David tended his father's sheep, slew the lion and the bear and learned of God's power to deliver. David composed his first immortal Psalms here and, as the ruddy shepherd lad, was anointed king of Israel by Samuel.

Centuries later, the prophet Micah predicted that the Messiah would be born in Bethlehem; so it was that Joseph and Mary, the peasant couple from Galilee, came for the greatest event of all time. Here, amid the strains of angelic music, the wonderful Child was born and the shepherds came as did the Wise Men of the east. Here all knelt and worshiped before Christ their Savior.

The light of Bethlehem, you see, is an ancient light—the light of sacred story, romance, prophecy, and glorious fulfillment. For the sake of the Christ Child, who was cradled in the manger of Bethlehem, we should relight the candle of hallowed memory in our hearts, and homes and churches. Only as the light of promise, hope and faith which streams from Bethlehem fills our minds and hearts will we know the meaning and reality of Christmas at all. "Remembrance, like a candle, shines brightest at Christmastime."

Candle of Love

There is also the candle of pure love. Bethlehem stands for the light of God's love for all mankind. Correggio and other artists painted masterpieces portraying light streaming from the manger and lighting the faces of Mary, Joseph, the shepherds and the Wise Men. God's gift of his Son reveals the love that is the light of the whole world. "God commendeth his own love toward us" in giving his Son to die for us. "For God so loved the world, that he gave his only begotten Son, that whosoever believeth on him should not perish, but have eternal life." Someone has given us a remarkable interpretation of God's gift of love in the following lines:

God: the greatest lover.
So loved: the greatest degree.
The world: the greatest company.
That he gave: the greatest act.
His only begotten Son: the greatest gift.
That whosoever: the greatest opportunity.
Believeth: the greatest simplicity.
In him: the greatest attraction.
Should not perish: the greatest promise.
But: the greatest difference.
Have: the greatest certainty.
Eternal life: the greatest possession.

We all need to light our candles at the fountain of light—divine love. "We love because he first loved us." Love to God and man is the light of the soul.

Love is also the light of our world. The way of love of Jesus of Bethlehem and Jerusalem is the only hope of our world. The love needed for the healing of the nations will never come from the great cities. It must come from the world's spiritual capital which is Bethlehem. "And nations will never come to thy light, and kings to the brightness of thy rising," so sang Isaiah. The love of God must be discovered, embraced and applied to all human problems and relationships if we are ever to have a new world of righteousness, peace and brotherhood. This love "beareth all things, believeth all things, hopeth all things, endureth all things." This love never faileth, but abideth forever.

Candle of True Worship

Then, there is the candle of true worship. The unfolding Nativity drama is an inspiring call to worship! The song of the angelic choir proclaims it: "Glory to God in the highest." The singular homage of the shepherds dramatizes it: "the shepherds returned, glorifying and praising God." The songs of praise and adoration of Elisabeth, Mary and Zacharias declare it. "And Mary said, My soul doth magnify the Lord, and my spirit hath rejoiced in God my Savior." Zacharias, filled with the Holy Spirit, said: "Blessed be the Lord, the God of Israel; for he hath visited and wrought redemption for his people." The noble example of the Wise Men enforces it: "and they fell down and worshiped him."

How shall we best light the candle of true worship? First of all, in our own hearts by remembering that God's gift of love is a personal gift to each one. No one else can receive the gift for you. No one can express gratitude and worship for the gift for you. You must light the candle of worship in your own heart. Each person must say to himself, in effect: "There is born to me this day in the city of David a Savior, who is Christ the Lord." "God so loved me that he gave his only begotten Son, that I, believing on him, might not perish but have eternal life." Thanks be unto God for his unspeakable gift—of Christ the Savior to me.

Candle of Perfect Peace

Finally, we include the candle of perfect peace. The light that is Bethlehem is the light of peace—for all believers and for the whole world. The prophet Isaiah said, "His name shall be called . . . the Prince of Peace." Micah prophesied: "And this man shall be our peace." Accordingly, the angelic chorus accompanied the tidings of the Messiah's birth with their song of glory and of peace, saying, "Glory to God in the highest, and on earth peace among men in whom he is well pleased." Later, the Prince of Peace taught his disciples, saying, "Blessed are the peacemakers: for they shall be called sons of God." And as his parting bequest to his friends, Christ said: "Peace I leave with you; my peace I give unto you; not as the world giveth, give I unto you. Let not your heart be troubled, neither let it be fearful."

Every part of our world needs the light of Christ's peace, and the beneficent works of his peacemakers. We need Christ's peace in our hearts and our homes; our churches and communities; our nation and the nations of the world. We need his peace in business and industry; in education and society; in politics and international relations. Only as the Prince of Peace shall rule in the councils of nations and in the affairs of men, will the star of hope burn brightly in the night sky of a weary world.

Fellow Christians, as we light these candles from Bethlehem, receiving from Christ the fullness of his truth and grace, let us remember his words: "I am the light of the world: he that followeth me shall not walk in the darkness, but shall have the light of life." And let us seek to carry out the commission he has laid upon us when He said: "Ye are the light of the world . . . Even so let your light shine before men; that they may see your good works, and glorify your Father who is in heaven." And as our prayer, let us repeat the words of John Masefield:

> Light comfort you,
> Light gladden you,
> Light bless you,
> Light fill your years
> And through you
> Lighten the world.

Painting opposite:
FLIGHT INTO EGYPT
Bartolomeo E. Murillo
(Photo, Three Lions, Inc.)

"For unto us a child is born, unto us a son is given: and the government shall be upon his shoulder: and his name shall be called Wonderful, Counseller, The mighty God, The everlasting Father, The Prince of Peace" (Isaiah 9:6).

The Gospel According to Luke and Matthew

And it came to pass in those days, that there went out a decree from Caesar Augustus, that all the world should be taxed. And all went to be taxed, every one into his own city. And Joseph also went up from Galilee, out of the city of Nazareth, into Judaea, unto the city of David, which is called Bethlehem; (because he was of the house and lineage of David:) To be taxed with Mary his espoused wife, being great with child. And so it was, that, while they were there, the days were accomplished that she should be delivered. And she brought forth her first born son, and wrapped him in swaddling clothes, and laid him in a manger; because there was no room for them in the inn.

And there were in the same country shepherds abiding in the field, keeping watch over their flock by night. And, lo, the angel of the Lord came upon them, and the glory of the Lord shone round about them: and they were sore afraid. And the angel said unto them, Fear not: for, behold, I bring you good tidings of great joy, which shall be to all people. For unto you is born this day in the city of David a Saviour, which is Christ the Lord. And this shall be a sign unto you; Ye shall find the babe wrapped in swaddling clothes, lying in a manger. And suddenly there was with the angel a multitude of the heavenly host praising God, and saying, Glory to God in the highest, and on earth peace, good will toward men.

And it came to pass, as the angels were gone away from them into heaven, the shepherds said one to another, Let us now go even unto Bethlehem, and see this thing which is come to pass, which the Lord hath made known unto us. And they came with haste, and found Mary, and Joseph, and the babe lying in a manger. And when they had seen it, they made known abroad the saying which was told them concerning this child. And all they that heard it wondered at those things which were told them by the shepherds.

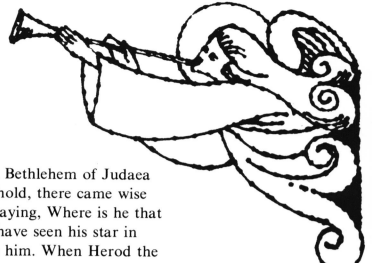

Now when Jesus was born in Bethlehem of Judaea in the days of Herod the king, behold, there came wise men from the east to Jerusalem, saying, Where is he that is born King of the Jews? for we have seen his star in the east, and are come to worship him. When Herod the king had heard these things, he was troubled, and all Jerusalem with him. And when he had gathered all the chief priests and scribes of the people together, he demanded of them where Christ should be born. And they said unto him, In Bethlehem of Judaea; for thus it is written by the prophet, And thou Bethlehem, in the land of Juda, art not the least among the princes of Juda: for out of thee shall come a Governor, that shall rule my people Israel.

Then Herod, when he had called the wise men, inquired of them diligently what time the star appeared. And he sent them to Bethlehem, and said, Go and search diligently for the young child; and when ye have found him, bring me word again, that I may come and worship him also. When they had heard the king, they departed; and lo, the star, which they saw in the east, went before them, till it came and stood over where the young child was. When they saw the star, they rejoiced with exceeding great joy.

And when they were come into the house, they saw the young child with Mary his mother, and fell down and worshiped him: and when they had opened their treasures, they presented unto him gifts: gold, and frankincense and myrrh. And being warned of God in a dream that they should not return to Herod, they departed into their own country another way. And when they were departed, behold, the angel of the Lord appeareth to Joseph in a dream, saying, Arise, and take the young child and his mother, and flee in Egypt, and be thou there until I bring thee word: for Herod will seek the young child to destroy him. When he arose, he took the young child and his mother by night, and departed into Egypt: And was there until the death of Herod: that it might be fulfilled which was spoken of the Lord by the prophet, saying, Out of Egypt have I called my son.

The Meaning of Christmas

Wise men came from the East, perhaps Persia. They saw the Babe — a Babe whose tiny hands were not quite long enough to touch the huge heads of the cattle, and yet hands that were steering the reins that keep the sun, moon, and stars in their orbits. Shepherds came, and they saw baby lips that did not speak, and yet lips that might have articulated the secret of every living man that hour. They saw a baby brow under which was a mind and intelligence compared with which the combined intelligences of Europe and America amount to naught.

One silent night, out over the white-chalked hills of Bethlehem, came a gentle cry. The great ones of the earth did not hear it, for they could not understand how an Infant could be greater than a man. At the Christ Child's birth, only two groups of people heard that cry: the Shepherds, who knew they did not know anything; and the Wise Men, who knew they did not know everything. Let us reach out at this Holy Christmas season to accept Christ with humility and love.

Fulton J. Sheen

Photo, Three Lions, Inc.

ADORATION OF THE SHEPHERDS, Bartolomeo E. Murillo

It Is Coming Tonight!

The earth has grown old
  with its burden of care,
But at Christmas it always is young.
The heart of the jewel
  burns lustrous and fair,
And its soul full of music
  breaks forth on the air
When the song of the angels is sung.

It is coming, old earth,
  it is coming tonight;
On the snowflakes which cover thy sod,

The feet of the Christ Child
  fall gently and white,
And the voice of the Christ Child
  tells out with delight
That mankind are the children of God.

On the sad and the lonely,
  the wretched and poor,
That voice of the Christ Child shall fall;
And to every blind wanderer opens the door
Of a hope which he dared
  not to dream of before,
With a sunshine of welcome for all.

The feet of the humblest
  may walk in the field
Where the feet of the holiest have trod;
This, this is the marvel
  to mortals revealed,
When the silvery trumpets
  of Christmas have pealed,
That mankind are the children of God.

Phillips Brooks